Sentimental Stories

ENRIQUE GÓMEZ CARRILLO (1873-1927) was a Guatemalan man of letters and diplomat, who associated and wrote about many famous writers of his day, including Oscar Wilde and Émile Zola. A prominent journalist, he contributed to numerous newspapers, in Spain, Argentina and Cuba, and was the author of over seventy books. Among his works of fiction were *Maravillas, novela funambulesca* (1906), and *El evangelio del Amor* (1922).

JESSICA SEQUEIRA is a writer and translator currently living in Santiago de Chile. Her works include the novel *A Furious Oyster* (Dostoyevsky Wannabe), the collection of stories *Rhombus and Oval* (What Books) and the collection of essays *Other Paradises: Poetic Approaches to Thinking in a Technological Age* (Zero Books). Her translations into English include Adolfo Couve's *When I Think of My Missing Head*, Hilda Mundy's *Pyrotechnics*, Liliana Colanzi's *Our Dead World*, Maurice Level's *The Gates of Hell*, Sara Gallardo's *Land of Smoke*, Teresa Wilms Montt's *In the Stillness of Marble*, and an anthology of stories by contemporary Chilean writers.

ENRIQUE GÓMEZ CARRILLO

Sentimental Stories

TRANSLATED AND WITH AN INTRODUCTION BY
JESSICA SEQUEIRA

Contents

Introduction:
Sentimentality in Excess

WHO was Enrique Gómez Carrillo? Biographies of the writer describe him as a man born in Guatemala but more comfortable in France, a dandy who fought twenty to thirty duels, an empathetic cosmopolitan observer of Jews, a recorder of sensation, a scribbler of combative articles, a sympathizer of the Guatemalan dictator Manuel Estrada Cabrera, a neurasthenic who bounced between depression and euphoria, a Don Juan who pursued female writers and divas, a chronicler of the first world war, a friend of Rubén Darío and Paul Verlaine, and a devoted if very difficult husband.

He was, perhaps, all of these things and none of them, performing his own personality yet not comfortable in any one role. The piled-up, frenetic quality of everything he did—there are so many books (a Spanish edition of collected works comes to twenty-six volumes), so many travels, so many women, so many opinions, so many sensuous descriptions—can be overwhelming.

Where to plunge into his work? What interested Gómez Carillo most in all of the pages he churned out, and what interests us? Studies of Gómez Carrillo have tended to focus on his non-fiction *crónicas*, not only because they make up the bulk of his work and were what brought him fame during his period, but also because they provide an interesting, prolific and ongoing account of his decades spent in Europe, the East and Latin America, through international crises and deep changes in artistic tendencies.

This book, a selection of nine stories, is a different cut, taken from the rich storytelling marrow of his work. Here is Gómez Carrillo not explicitly provoking or registering the cultural mores around him, but creating his own fictional worlds,in doing so casting his interests and preoccupations into a kind of relief, denuded of the costumbrist jewelry so present in his journalistic endeavors.

One such concern, reflected in the title itself of this collection, is sentimentality. In Gómez Carrillo's world, precisely on the knife edge of the nineteenth and twentieth centuries—*Sentimental Stories* was originally published in 1900—to be sentimental was to be not only emotionally inclined but also psychologically weak, prone to mental degeneration. The title is not so much romantic as it is a kind of warning: in the stories of the Guatemelan author, sentimentality inevitably produces great suffering for the stories' protagonists, often resulting in madness. The solitary figures who fill his tales try to live bohemian lives outside the bourgeois system, but their incorrigible sentimentality leads them to downfall by various routes.

Desire and insanity both rear their heads, as characters talk to themselves and pursue strange obsessions.

The bourgeoisie is painted in bleak colors, as hypocrites: for isn't it better to feel something than simply to count down the days of a staid life? Gómez Carrillo repeatedly has his characters ask this question, but judging by their fates, the answer isn't obvious. Religion and psychological analysis come in for an acid bath of irony too, as mere institutions of illusion.

This is a novena of stories, and the story ends with a novena; but if a prayer cannot save these characters, one might well ask what redemption is possible. Fulfillment in erotic love and suffering in intense anguish are the two states portrayed again and again in these tales, with the pendulum swinging from one to the other. The "sentimental" state is a temporary in-between, and never lasts for long.

Gómez Carrillo's own style is overwrought, but within a classical framework. His stories are highly formal in their structure: stories within stories, fragments that are purposely-broken parts of a whole. He uses the diary form to great effect, as well as the fairy tale. The stylistic precision of his work is emphasized by the fact that his stories bear dedications to other writers. It is clear they seek to be admired as beautiful works of art in themselves: lapidary arrangements of words, precious stones.

Gómez Carrillo was born in Guatemala City in 1873 and died in Paris in 1927. He was an autodidact. As he recounts in *El despertar del alma* [The Awakening of the Soul], from a very young age he dedicated himself to journalism. When Rubén Darío founded the newspaper *El Correo de la Tarde*, Gómez Carrillo was one of its editors.

In 1891 the president of Guatemala, Manuel Lisandro Barillas, awarded him a scholarship to study in Spain. As a newspaper correspondent for *El Liberal*, he began a series of journeys through countries in Europe, North Africa, Asia and America. He lived in different European capitals, above all Paris and Madrid, where he directed the modernist magazine *El Nuevo Mercurio* (1907) and *Cosmópolis*, a magazine of literature and criticism for America and Spain (1919-1921). He was also a consul during the Manuel Estrada Cabrera government in Madrid, London, Hamburg and Paris.

Gómez Carrillo was married three times, to the Peruvian writer Aurora Cáceres, the Spanish actress Raquel Meller and the Salvadoran-French writer and artist Consuelo Suncin de Sandoval-Cardenas, later Comtesse de Saint-Exupéry (of *The Little Prince*). At one point the head of the German secret services accused him, along with Meller, of giving up the famous spy Mata Hari to the French during World War I, which Gómez Carrillo denied, though he took the opportunity to write a popular book about the dancer. In Paris, at a young age, Gómez Carrillo acquired syphilis, a common but incurable disease in his circles, for which he would receive injections of blood, thought to be useful at the time.

His literary style is considered "modernist" in its use of poetic prose, high emotion and choice of themes that challenged the basis of civilization. He was influenced by café tertulias and by writers who were also pioneering new styles—besides Darío and Verlaine, his friends in Paris included Jean Moréas and Leconte de Lisle, and he met James Joyce, Oscar Wilde and Émile Zola, among others. His pieces express a taste for traveling, bohemian life, exotic places, adventurous loves, eroticism and sensuousness of all kinds. Prologues to his works were written by important writers like Benito Pérez Galdós and Maurice Maeterlinck.

Famous for his impressionistic accounts, for which he gained the nickname "Príncipe de las Crónicas" [Prince of the Chronicles], Gómez Carrillo published five books of journalistic pieces. He also wrote the following novels: *Tres novelas inmorales (Del amor, del dolor y del vicio)* [Three Immoral Novels (Of Love, Pain and Vice)] (1898), *Bohemia sentimental* [Sentimental Bohemia] (1900), *Pobre clown* [Poor Clown] (1899), and *El evangelio del amor* [The Gospel of Love] (1922).

Further volumes of his chronicles and travel impressions include *La Rusia actual* [Modern Day Russia] (1906), *La Grecia eterna* [Eternal Greece] (1908), *El Japón heroico y galante* [Heroic and Gallant Japan] (1912), *Jerusalén y la Tierra Santa* [Jerusalem and the Holy Land] (1912), *La sonrisa de la esfinge* [The Smile of the Sphinx] (1913), *El encanto de Buenos Aires* [The Charm of Buenos Aires] (1914) and *Fez, la andaluza* [Fez, the Andalucian] (1926). Among his war chronicles are *Campos de batalla y campos de ruinas* [Fields of Battle and Fields of Ruins] (1915) and *En las trincheras* [In the Trenches] (1916).

As a critic of literature and art, Gómez Carrillo wrote *Sensaciones de Arte* [Sensations of Art](1893), *Literatura Extranjera. Estudios cosmopolitas* [Foreign

Literature: Cosmopolitan Studies] (1895), *El modern-ismo* [Modernism] (1905), *Las cien obras maestras de la literatura universal* [One Hundred Masterpieces of World Literature] (1926) and *La nueva literatura francesa* [The New French Literature] (1927).

Other books of his include: *El misterio de la vida y de la muerte de Mata-Hari* [The Mystery of the Life and Death of Mata Hari] (1923) and *La verdad sobre Guatemala* [The Truth About Guatemala] (1906).

In 1906, the Académie Française awarded him the Montyon Prize for his translation into French of his own work *El alma japonesa* [The Japanese Soul], and a second time in 1917 for the translation of his work *En el corazón de la tragedia* [At the Heart of the Tragedy].

When he died, Gómez Carrillo was buried in Père Lachaise, and the epitaph in Spanish on his tomb can be translated as: "Always alert in the midst of so many sleeping things."

Two physical fetishes reappear in Gómez Carillo's tales, symbols of the sentimental contradiction between emotion and intellect in his work. The first is a blonde wig which, resting in a shop window, represents another life for sale, exotic and glamorous, an artificial existence removed from the "real" of the here and now.

The blonde wig is a rarity given that most heads are dark, a bewitching abstraction, a coy object that considers the natural to be rather dull. (Isn't that so, darling?) Today we think of Marilyn, Lana Turner, Brigitte Bardot:

the inhuman gleam of polyvinyl makes no pretense to be authentic. The blonde wig is affectedness itself, like a poem about a kiss without any real kiss. Yet its presence also suggests the possibility of a woman and carnal love. In ancient Greece, prostitutes would often dye their hair blonde or wear a flaxen wig.

The second object to appear in these stories is the tanagra figurine, a tiny woman of classical elegance and white purity, a slim *objet d'art*. A formal beauty with no drape or gesture out of place, this is an item to be contemplated with cool pleasure, not sensuous but intellectual, an ideal miniature. A character wracked by desire claims to have this figurine at the "bottom of his soul," and he may not be wrong, but this beauty is seen to have limits. In another story, the same figure is coveted by an academic, to be "lined up in a mute and evocative phalanx"; ultimately, however, desire wins out, and he is drawn to the more earthly intimations of the blonde wig. The tanagra figurine may be a beautiful woman, but it cannot be loved.

In *The Meaning of Art*, Herbert Read wrote that: "The significance of the Northern mode lies precisely in its life-denying qualities, its completely abstract character; and in this character, these qualities, we must see a reflection of the spiritual life of these Northern people—'the heavily oppressed inner life of Northern humanity', as Worringer has called it."

The categories of North and South are so vague they are not helpful as anthropological categories, but their dichotomy does illuminate some interesting ways of thinking about artistic forms, if geography isn't taken literally.

The cold North, according to Read, prefers the unnatural in art; the angular, rigid, abnormal and strange are seen as more interesting than the easy organic pleasures of the warm South. Northern artists turn their eye upon the world to experience it as a relationship between discrete objects and the angles between them. Southern artists, on the other hand, see the world as a vital force that fills all things. The Northern form of being is analytical, a psychology of thought, a calculating mentality that seeks new relations between objects, a rearrangement of the chessboard by which the artist wishes to view reality in novel ways. The Southern form of being gathers experience without seeking to correct or reorder it, simply allowing it to flow.

Yet perhaps an intermediate state exists between Read's dichotomies, that of the Southern-type artist who transforms into a Northern-type artist, or vice versa. This might result in a formalist shaping of the ugly, kitsch, sentimental and mindlessly organic. A long journey of rejecting the other pole, to ultimately embrace it, would result in a sensuality that is no longer simple, but a mask of simplicity.

Gómez Carrillo is a writer of the south who crystallized his sentiments into northern structures, or perhaps a writer of the north whose art is filled with southern life force. His life and form of writing embody as many ambiguities and contradictions as do the blonde wig and tanagra figurine, in an androgyny of style that pirouettes on the fine line between decadent sentimentality and modernist formalism, the nineteenth and the twentieth century, south and north, eros and anguish, chaos and formality.

A Guatemalan living in Paris, Gómez Carillo was a cold and emotionally astute artist who embalmed hot states of anguish into tales of cold perfection. The contradiction is in the very title of the work in which these *Sentimental Tales* were originally published: *Almas y cerebros* [Souls and Minds] —a volume divided into two sections, the first "Sentimental Tales" and the second "Parisian Intimacies," consisting of non-fiction pieces about writers such as Jean Lorrain, J.-K. Huysmans and August Strindberg.

Translating these stories, I kept thinking about the ways that Gómez Carrillo's work captures a certain tone of emotional reaction, a sensibility of "too much." Characters live in their own fairy tale or illusory mental realities, and are willing to kill and be killed for love. Gómez Carrillo seems aware of his own extremity, and there is often humor in the cruelty of his sufferers' plights and delusions, and in the portrayal of characters from the mistaken cuckold to the hack writer.

Sentimentality and excess were both important elements in Gómez Carrillo's life, but it remains ambiguous as to whether Gómez Carrillo personally experienced this sentimental excess. His stories are fraught with descriptions of strident and anguished emotion, but perhaps he discovered a certain sentimental attraction in excess itself. Perhaps he found delight, glory, beauty and freedom in exaggeration and surfeit, dissolution and extravagance; perhaps, in love with literature, with all his wits about him, he accordingly adjusted his life.

—Jessica Sequeira

Bibliography

Cáceres, Aurora. *Mi vida con Enrique Gómez Carrillo*. Editorial Renacimiento, 1929.

Carrillo, Jaime Barrios. "Enrique Gómez Carrillo: el mago de las letras." *Revista Luna Park*, no. 14. 2013.

Castillo Puche, José Luis. "Gómez Carrillo tópico del modernismo." *El País*. 11 April 1986.

Ehrlicher, Hanno. "Enrique Gómez Carrillo en la red cosmopolita del modernismo." *Iberoamericana*, no. 15, 60, pp. 41-60. 2015.

Feria, Miguel Ángel. "Enrique Gómez Carrillo y el cisma poético del modernismo hispánico." *Revista Letral* (Universidad de Granada), no. 19, pp. 83-97. 2018.

Fernández, Juan Carlos Mateos. "Cuestión de honor Los periodistas se baten en duelo." *Historia y Comunicación Social*, no. 3, pp. 232 - 341. 1998.

Gómez Carrillo, Enrique. *Almas y Cerebros*, Garnier Hermanos, 1900.

Kronik, John. "Enrique Gómez Carrillo, francophile propagandist." *Symposium*, no. 21, pp. 50-60. 1967.

Mendoza, Juan Manuel. *Enrique Gómez Carrillo: estudio crítico-biográfico; su vida, su obra y su época*. 1946.

Siskind, Mariano. *Cosmopolitan Desires: Global Modernity and World Literature in Latin America.* 2014.

Torres Espinoza, Edelberto. *Enrique Gómez Carrillo, el cronista errante.* Librería Escolar, 1956.

Sentimental Stories

The Fatal Return

I

AFTER having hesitated a whole week, Mauricio decided, one night of idleness and melancholy, to undertake what he called "a work of amorous charity."

"Poor boys," he said to himself, "it's necessary to be good to them!"

And he started to search in the depths of a little marble trunk, a dashing and perfumed reliquary, for the letters that Luisa had written to him in other times, before he'd met Marcela, before she'd dined with Raúl, now already many months ago, many months . . . almost a year. There all of them were—the poor letters!—tied with a green ribbon, giving off a scent of withered roses and dead kisses.

. . . Truly it made no sense for that idiot Raúl to despair over ten or twelve pieces of paper that would never be worth a thing!

Mauricio seized the packet, put it into the waist pocket of his topcoat and came down, smiling and light, to the door of his hotel, where the carriage had been waiting for him for half an hour.

II

When he saw her again, on her way to Luisa's house, in the same *coupé* as always, at the same hour as in former times, Mauricio experienced a strange feeling, something at the same time spiteful curiosity and vague sadness.

What was she going to say to him when she saw him arrive? . . . Would she cry? . . . Would she be more beautiful? . . . Would she have gotten fat? . . . Would she be disdainful, or indifferent? . . . No; indifferent, no; their love had been too intense, too sincere, to disappear completely without leaving, in the depths of that heart that had been all fire a year ago, what people often call embers.

Nevertheless, although he had also loved her a great deal for six months, afterward he had forgotten her almost completely, to the point of not thinking of her except when he had truly nothing else to think about or was sick and alone. But women forget with less ease than men . . . What's more, he had a thousand worries and a thousand things to do, while she, withdrawn and sickly, hardly left her house . . .

He also had the excuse of Marcela—Marcela, beautiful Marcela, the most alluring actress in France—while she was reduced to the insipid adoration of Raúl, a poor boy who had the happiness of people who lack amorous history.

"What a fool! . . ."

Mauricio spoke to himself out loud, as if in a dream:

"... This one sure deserves his luck ... To be called Raúl de la Siserane, to be nephew to the Count of Labadi, to possess a hundred thousand escudos in assets, yet to want to marry a girl who has no other gift than to be consumptive and to be have been the student of many professors of love ...! And the curious thing is that the idiot isn't even crazy: he talks the same way as everyone does, and goes to the Club, and has great dealings in business, and wins at the tables. Last night when we met at the Opera, I thought he'd impertinently remind me of my promise to return the letters to Luisa; on the contrary, he came to sit beside me, and in half an hour of pleasant chat made not the slightest allusion to the subject. Those degenerate boys who descend in a straight line from the gentlemen of Malta never lose their minds, and do everything methodically, in a bourgeois way, out of a healthy and paradoxical mental weakness ... Since Luisa doesn't want to marry the hundred thousand francs a year so long as I haven't returned her letters, the best thing would therefore be not to return them. The best for him. I prefer to be of use to this woman who, after all, knew how to love me so much, with such ardor, and who maybe later on, when Marcela ..."

The voice of the footman, who opened the door to say: "The gentleman has arrived", interrupted his monologue.

III

Before knocking on the bronze door that gave access to the garden, Mauricio stopped to see if the letters were really in his pocket. Immediately afterward, he arranged the knot in his tie and nervously smoothed his dress coat, like a student going on a date. The palms of his hands were damp.

Far away a clock chimed nine.

"Only nine? . . . Too early . . . Luisa could be still in the dining room. It's necessary to wait a few minutes, a quarter of an hour at least, until the moment for the visits arrives, all the visits . . ." Because now, in that house where he had previously been hers, he was only a vulgar friend, a friend like any other, without more rights than the baron of X . . . and without more duties than the marquises of H . . .

The idea that he could almost be a stranger in that place obsessed Mauricio. For the first time in his life, his passionate imagination made him see the thousand sad facets of an amorous existence:—"So, then, two hearts no longer recognize each other, after having been a single heart? And without apparent reason, without justification, almost without exhaustion, simply because . . . Would Marcela forget him too, tomorrow, like the others? . . . One night, all of a sudden, when his head began to lose hairs or cover itself with white strands, all of his current realities would turn into a terrible labyrinth of memories . . ."

A psychological curiosity made him smile: Who was going to be, much later—oh, much later! in old age—

his best memory of love? Julia, the granddaughter of the gentleman from Brumond? Or Ester, pretty Ester, always fresh and joyful? Or pale Luisa? No; it would be Marcela, the modern muse, the slender one, the sinner with immaculate curves! . . . His lips repeated Marcela's name; but at the bottom of his soul, a very thin and very white image, a nearly mystical Tanagra figurine, persisted . . .

IV

Mauricio entered the hall, and while the servant went to announce him, meticulously examined his surroundings. Nothing had changed there, neither the furniture, nor the tapestries, nor the paintings, nor the big lamps veiled by immense shades in muted colors, nor even the perfume, that indefinable perfume, misty, exotic and penetrating. Even the flowers that filled the vases on the hearth seemed the same as a year before.

Mauricio felt, at the bottom of his being, a gust of something very ardent and very sad, something like a wave of incomplete sighs, perhaps a germ of nostalgia.

Luisa entered at last, wrapped in a white silk dressing gown.

She hadn't changed either: the same fragile waist, the same blonde head of hair, thick, ample; the same sickly and almost transparent complexion of dull mother-of-pearl; the same dark eyes, well-defined, almost sunk in big blue undereye circles, and above all, the same adorable hands of a princess from a fantastic tale—tiny hands, long, tapering, unbelievable in their grace and refinement . . .

"I was expecting you," she said, as she came in.

And, as if it had just been a week since she'd last seen her former lover, she went on:

"What have you been doing? Why haven't you come?"

Mauricio didn't know how to reply. The friendly tone and familiar smile of his former girlfriend disconcerted him in a strange way. He would have liked to have handed her the letters and left, without speaking a word. But it was impossible. Something mysterious, something supernatural restrained him . . .

V

Was it the perfume of that all the furniture exuded? . . . or the unhealthy curiosity of returning to feel the old quivers? or the beauty of Luisa, that beauty of a dying flower, almost macabre in whiteness as if she were in a shroud, yet so sweet? . . . Mauricio felt his eyelids filling with tears. For two minutes—an eternity in an idyll—his lips could not move.

Then a mirage appeared before his vision . . . It was an extrordinary mirage, illuminated by the flickering lights of votive candles, embalmed with an aroma of incense that rose to his brain and formed, before his eyes, a dark little cloud in the depths of which was a hand that said farewell, a hand without rancor, a hand that went away after having called him, that went away little by little, disappearing slowly . . .

He couldn't take it anymore. He began to speak. And hardly understanding the true sense of what he was saying, obeying a secret sentiment, with an impulse never felt before, in a very soft voice, lowering his eyes:

"Forgive me!" he said. "Forgive me! I've been a fool and I've been vain. I've made you suffer, I haven't recognized your beauty . . . Forgive me, because the immense guilt of my pride is not entirely mine, and, in reality, is almost not mine at all but belongs to life itself, or to the light of the salons that prevented me from seeing into the depth of my soul, to the noise of the dances that overcame the voice of my heart. Forgive me because now in the silence of your existence I've heard myself, in the shadows of your gaze I've seen myself, and I understand that I'm worth less than you, less than the rest, less than everyone! . . ."

While Mauricio was speaking, Luisa stood up, and, with lips half-open, dry, trembling; with pupils looking at something distant; in an inscrutable and motionless posture she looked as if she were listening to something terrible and far away.

Mauricio went on:

"In the end, I've been nothing but an elegant toy of Destiny. I haven't been cruel since I've never known what cruelty was; I haven't perjured because I've always ignored the solemn grandeur of the oath . . . I've been a Faun of luxury, thoughtless and irresponsible . . . But today I feel able to begin my life again, to undertake a great experience, distance myself from Egoism and consecrate myself to true love, your love, Luisa, my Luisa; to adore you once again . . . to continue adoring you, to be yours

and make you mine . . . Say yes . . . say something . . .
say you forgive me, that you grant me permission to be
your slave . . ."

"No!" replied the pale shadow.

"No? Don't you believe me? . . . Then let me prove to
you that I'm no longer the same, that I've changed, that
I'm another and that I understand you. Let me be faithful
to you for a year, before you let me kneel at your feet to
receive a caress; make me wait, make me live . . . a month
. . . a year . . . five years . . . all of existence . . ."

"No! No!"

"I understand, Luisa: it's because you love the other,
Raúl, the good lover who saw how to approach you and
who serves as a nurse to dress the wounds of your soul . . .
Isn't it true this is what he's for? . . ."

"Go away; don't torture me; don't ever come back."

"Go? You want me to leave?"

"Yes; go away; leave."

"Because you love the other, because you adore him
. . . isn't that true?"

"Go away."

"Tell me you love him."

"Yes, but go away; don't make me suffer . . . yes . . ."

Automatically, as if moved by a spring of insulted
vanity, Mauricio set off toward the door of the hall and
opened it abruptly. When he turned around to close it
behind him, he heard the dry sound, the mortal blow of
a body as it collapsed . . . and without realizing what he
was doing, shaking, upset, faltering, with hands clenched
and forehead covered in cold sweat, he fled . . .

Cleopatra's Wig

For D. J.-M. Herrera Irigoyen

I

TEODORO, the unknown old poet, had the habit of stopping, on his way to the library, in front of all the window displays in Our Lord Street.

First he visited the shop windows of the bookseller: he looked at the new books, felt moved by rare editions, and picked out the ideal place where his great poem on ancient love, his *Cleopatra Victrix*, would be exhibited later on, when it was printed . . . when would his poem be printed? . . . "Modern editors lack taste and talent." Hachette didn't accept anyone's verses and Quintín had laughed at his style; the rest didn't even want to take the trouble to receive him . . .

Then he had a look at the bronzes of the antique shop: bronzes in general, without any merit; an immense pile of figures from the beginning of the century, with great pretensions to classicism, all wrapped in peplos garments, shod in sandals and brutal in the false delicacy of their proportions. Only ten or twelve Kanephoros, Tanagra figurines that were also imitations but artistic ones, small and slim, seemed worthy of being contemplated with pleasure. If he had possessed the money, he would have bought them all to put on his work table, lined up in a mute and evocative phalanx . . . he would buy them later on, when an editor printed his poem . . .

After that he inspected the furniture of the cabinet-maker, the diamonds of the jeweler, the portraits of the photographer and even the wigs of the hairdresser.

At last, when the clock struck nine, nine exactly, he quickened his step; a quarter of an hour later made his entrance into the public reading hall, where he gathered the documents necessary to finish his new book, *The Psychological Evolution of the Kiss.*

II

Teodoro Sylarus was what in French is called *un raté*, but he was a *raté* without bile and without rancor. When by chance one of his old classmates managed to achieve fame in the world of letters, the poor author of *Cleopatra Victrix*, far from feeling jabs of envy, was sincerely happy, and from the depths of his heart celebrated the triumph of another with true enthusiasm. Never did he make a complaint against his peers; never did he show the least desire to obtain a similar position. Did others achieve fame and money? So much the better. He'd achieve it too . . .

The only human beings who inspired dislike in him were editors.

"The editors of our time," he often said, "are worse than those of before, or at least different. In other times, the man who consecrated himself of his own accord to printing the books of others was a real dilettante who read manuscripts conscientiously, and knew how to understand what he read. Today the editor is a merchant of bestsellers, who'd never dream of reading two verses by an unknown author, and who reduces his priesthood to requesting novels or poems from those with at least one scandal in the press. For my part I will not make any scandal, but I will keep looking with patience for the publisher I must eventually come across. I will find him; why shouldn't I find him?"

And without losing any of his illusions, without being intimidated and without losing hope, he continued to work.

His *Cleopatra Victrix*—ten entire years of labor—was a long dithyramb in tercets, in which the queen of Egypt appeared in all the symbolic glory of her beauty, like a tamer of wills, an image of supreme and irresistible seduction. The poet hadn't wanted to speak of the beloved of Antony and of Caesar alone, but of all feminine beauty. To carry out his allegorical ideal, he attributed to his vanquishing Cleopatra the cruel gifts of Salomé and the divine majesty of the Greek Venus. Melted into a single body of blonde flesh, the three goddesses of voluptuousness formed a monster of disturbing beauty, full of feline hypocrisy, idle majesty and bloodthirsty attraction.

"The Trinity of Love," said the poet.

III

In the *Psychological Evolution of the Kiss*, the dominant note was historical subtlety. Teodoro Silarus had studied all the works related to love, from the books of the Old Testament to the speeches of Psycharis and the novels of the Goncourt brothers.

"In these works," he said to the few charitable beings who consented to hear his speeches, "I have found many contradictions and many errors. Pischaris, for instance, in his study read before the Court of Athens, claims that the kiss on the lips, the kiss on the mouth, is a modern invention, and that it was used for the first time in a scene in *Paolo e Francesca* by Dante Alighieri, a Florentine poet of the Middle Ages, when in reality it dates back to far before the Christian Era. The Book of Tobit in Chapters IX and X, and the Book of Ruth in Verse 14 of Chapter I, already speak to us of the kiss on the mouth and beard as a sign of friendship, or love. The true origin of the osculation is found in the Holy Scriptures. The first kiss is the one that, according to Job, primitive men sent toward the heavenly bodies, bearing their hands to their lips and then raising them to the heavens: *si vidi solem aut lunam et osculatum sum manum meam ore meo*. In the New Testament, Saint Paul recommends to the faithful that they greet one another through an osculation: *Salutate invicen osculo sancto*. Later, the Christian division of kisses is established into the kiss of the altar, the kiss of peace and the kiss of hands or feet; but, as is correct, two

32

of these kisses no longer exist, as Pope Innocent III saw it necessary to suppress the second due to abuses of the clergy in his time. In Greece the kiss was a sign of ordinary sympathy. In Eastern countries, according to what Niebuhr claims in his very interesting account of his travels, the most vulgar kiss is that which men give to women on the knees. In the fifteenth century, in Europe, gentlemen greeted ladies by means of a kiss on the lips, a promiscuous custom that made the great Montaigne say, in a beautiful chapter of the *Essays*, that his pretty contemporaries were the most wretched beings on the planet, when the man who greeted them was old or ugly. Later on, this privilege of kissing female mouths was especially reserved to cardinals, who had the right to *greet on the lips the Queen herself our lady*. John the Second, a modern Latin poet who in the mid-sixteenth century wrote in the language of Lazio, with Petronian grace and a correctness worthy of Virgil, divides the scale of human love into nineteen kisses: the first of which is that of childhood and the last of which is the one that a man and a woman give each other in bed, after mutual possession. In the eighteenth century, the kiss came to lose its religious character, due to the libidinous frivolity of customs; and although it seems strange, the only one who saw it as a sacred caress was Voltaire. In our century, the osculation has recovered something of its former character, but my book refers above all to the periods that have fallen definitively under the domain of historical science."

IV

Beyond his poetic work and his erudite speculations, Teodoro busied himself with giving Latin classes to the students of three or four religious schools, and the little these classes produced for him gave him the amount necessary so his family did not die of hunger.

. . . For the author of *Cleopatra Victrix* had a family: a wife and two sons. He had got married, without knowing how, between two cantos of his poem, to a somewhat faded dressmaker whose profile had seemed Greek to him one spring afternoon. And his ten years of conjugal life had been neither joyful nor miserable.

The only thing that sometimes seemed to him disagreeable was that his wife had false ideas about education, saying to him in moments of poverty:

"When the kids are grown, I'll make sure that I teach them to work seriously, so that they can enter a trade."

But at heart Teodoro was sure that his heirs would dedicate themselves to Latin and Greek, just as he had, and this certainty consoled him after the foolish remarks of his other half.

V

One morning, after having looked at the eternal incunabula of the bookseller and the unchanging figurines of the antiques dealer, a wig called his attention in the window of the barbershop. It was a woman's wig, blonde, very blonde, dark blonde, Venetian blonde, with tones of polished copper, silky, enormous, splendid. For half an hour his eyes did not tire of admiring this wig without a head, which for him had something enigmatic about it that made him think vaguely of Cleopatra, of Salomé and the decapitation of Saint John the Baptist.

The next day he almost passed over the curiosities in all the other shop windows to spend his entire hour of idleness in almost amorous contemplation of the wig. For several weeks the shop window of the barbershop was for him a shrine and place of pilgrimage.

The great unmoving wig attracted him, subjugated him, obsessed him.

A fanciful idea took hold of his brain: How had that divine wig been able to arrive there, after so many centuries, traveling through so much space? Because it was, there was no doubt about it, the mane of the Queen, the mane of Cleopatra, the sweet mane in which there could still be seen the metallic gleams of weapons, the vibrations of insatiable and proud love, the tender gestures of the imperial slave of the East, all the gifts, in short, all the perfume and perversity of the ancient seductress! . . . Marc Antony had caressed her, and his ardent fingers of a lover and warrior had sunk into those strands of desert light, savage and refined! . . . O divine wig, relic of eternal love, fragment of ancient life, trophy of dead beauty! . . .

VI

With the aim of knowing precisely what color the wig of the Egyptian queen had been, Teodoro embarked on new and profound historical studies. He read a great number of Latin, French and English comedies, quoted by Stafer in his dramatic bibliography on Cleopatra; he read, with more attention than before, the works of Plutarch, those of Marmontel, those of Montreux, those of Théophile Gautier, those of Houssaye, etc. Nowhere did he find a serious clue that could serve as decisive proof. Some claimed that the wig had been dark-haired; others, the majority, that it had been blonde, but no one supported their assertions with formal documents. Then the poor poet turned to paintings, to the ancient pictures above all. *The Death of Cleopatra*, by Dominichino; *Cleopatra*, by Guido; *Cleopatra Stepping Ashore at Tarsa*, by Claude Lorrain; *Cleopatra* by Gerard de Lairesse; all the images of the queen to be found in the Louvre or in museums of reproductions were examined by Teodoro, who, convinced at last that every artist had attributed to the royal wig the color that best fit his own tastes, abandoned his studies and continued to believe that his intuition of an ideal lover had not deceived him, and that what he saw every morning in the shop window of Our Lord Street was the true mane whose perfume had captivated Caesar and driven Marc Antony mad.

VII

One day, leaving the library, he met with one of those old classmates of his who did not know Greek, or Hebrew, or even Latin, yet had achieved a certain literary notoriety.

"What's going on with you?"

"Nothing, I'm the same as ever: and you?"

"Me too, same as ever, always rowing in the galley of letters, as our rhetoric professor put it. Just now I've just been named director of *The Star of the Century*, a magazine that pays, my man, a *rara avis in terra* as you would say . . . By the way, why don't you bring me an article or story?"

The author of *Cleopatra* didn't write articles or stories.

"Do you want a poem about antiquity?"

"No; no verses: verses don't pay."

"Then what about a psychological and historical study of the kiss, something your readers will enjoy; it's not long, four issues, five at most . . . would you like it?"

"I think so; but four or five numbers, that's almost a serialized novel . . . how much do you want for your history?"

"Whatever you will give me, my man, anything. You already know that I have no right to be demanding."

"Forty *duros*?"

"Yes, whatever you say."

"Then we have a deal: forty *duros* and come by on Tuesday; not the next; the one after, in fourteen days. Goodbye."

"Goodbye."

VII

It was the first time that a work of his was going to be printed, what a triumph! Yet the poet didn't seem very satisfied. If it had been the other, the *Cleopatra Vitrix*, his delight would have been boundless; but the *Evolution*, a purely erudite study . . . it wasn't truly worth it.

When he came home he examined his manuscript. The book was already finished; all that was missing was the chapter titles, the historical index and versions of the Greek and Latin quotations. Two weeks of labor and all would be ready.

He began to prepare, then, his great folios of enquiries; he put on his glasses and set to work. And to be more sure of not breaking his word, he decided not to go to the schools where he taught until he'd delivered the manuscript.

During those two weeks of joblessness, bread wasn't very abundant on his table. But fourteen days go by quickly, and in the garret of the poet all consoled their appetites thinking that "Tuesday after next" wouldn't take long to arrive, that it would arrive with forty *duros*, and that with forty *duros* would come a feast.

The anticipated Tuesday arrived. The author of the *Psychological Evolution of the Kiss* delivered his original manuscript and collected the sum agreed, in two blue notes from the Bank of France.

VIII

For what reason, leaving the editorial office of the *Star of the Century*, did Teodoro seem unhappy? Had they given him a poor reception? Had they requested him to change some of his philosophical conclusions so as not to upset skittish readers? No. The unhappiness of the

poet didn't have any definite cause, and more than unhappiness, it was a distant sadness, a nervous unease, an
indefinable preoccupation, a nostalgic longing for poetry
and passion.

To calm himself he'd have liked to have moved a great
deal, a very great deal; to walk until he reached the Bois
de Boulogne and return on foot. But this was impossible,
because his wife and his children were waiting for the
forty *duros* to buy lunch, and three in the afternoon had
already struck on all the clocks.

For the first time in his life, he understood that the
burden of family weighed too heavily on him, and that
the bourgeois tyranny of material life was the most terrible of all tyrannies.

"In the Middle Ages," he thought, "the conditions
of existence were less vulgar! . . . Who wouldn't prefer
to have been born in the Middle Ages, in the time of
Petrarch! . . . Or in antiquity—in Rome, in Byzantium,
in Egypt . . . in Egypt above all, in the divine period when
the queen's carriage hugged the coastline of the beaches,
its immense purple veils flapping in the wind! . . . Oh,
the Queen! . . . And to think that the barbarian Pascal
could speak of her goddess's profile without an artist's
enthusiasm, without any fervor whatsoever, considering
it to be only a political instrument . . ."

Reasoning in this way, he arrived at Our Lord Street
and went straight to the shop window of the hairdresser.
The mane of his daydreams hadn't changed place: there
it was, the same as before, more beautiful even, more
blonde, more provocative than ever, with its gleams of
dark bronze, shining under the sun . . .

The poor poet contemplated it lovingly for ten minutes. Then he imagined buying it to have the right to caress it whenever he liked, not only with his gaze but also with his hands, just as Caesar and Marc Antony had. How much could it cost? Three, four, five *duros*? Perhaps ten . . . But what would ten *duros* mean to a man who had forty? . . . And Cleopatra's wig was so beautiful!

He entered the store and asked the price.

"Forty *duros*, sir; it's a natural wig . . ."

Forty *duros*? . . . His fortune! . . . No, he couldn't, he shouldn't buy it; he had no right to dispose of all his money to pay for such madness, while his wife and children were fasting.

The hairdresser continued:

". . . A natural wig, guaranteed, authentic, the finest one can find; come touch, it feels like silk . . ."

The poet touched it piously. A diabolic shiver shook his entire body. But he couldn't, he couldn't, he couldn't . . . his family . . . lunch . . . dinner . . . Impossible!

". . . I'll put it in a box for you; here it is," the hairdresser went on.

"Impossible!" murmured the poet. "Impossible, impossible! No, no, I can't!"

But at the same time, without knowing what he was doing, automatically, in as if in a dream, he took from his pocket the two hundred-franc notes he'd just received and placed them on the hairdresser's counter.

Psychopathy

I

THAT afternoon my friends had already left, and in the café where we were all in the habit of drinking absinthe, only Doctor Lariviere remained, a tiresome old man to whom I'd hardly ever addressed a word.

For half an hour neither the doctor nor I opened our lips. He read *Le Temps* with meticulous attention; I quickly glanced over all the publications of the day, looking for something new, something that could interest me, something signed by a friend, something, in short, that wasn't the eternal article about the triple alliance, the French-Russian pact, or the question of the East and the European balance. But nothing: in the newspapers there wasn't a thing worth reading, not even a story of worldly scandal or a tale of a crime, nothing! And yet the doctor continued to read without lifting his eyes, without moving, as if he had in his hands a book by Edgar Poe or Balzac.

"What extraordinary adventure are you reading with such attention, Doctor?"

My question seemed to him, no doubt, very ironic. His reply was stiff:

"I'm reading," he said, "what I feel like."

"I understand," I went on, without giving way to anger, "but is what you're reading in *Le Temps* very interesting?"

"All the serious publications," he answered me, "are worthy of being read with interest; and if you don't find anything you like in either *La Liberté*, or *La Gazette*, or the *Journal des Débats*, the fault isn't with the editors of those newspapers, but with yourself, or, to put it a better way, with your illness."

"My illness?" The phrase seemed to me a curious one. What illness was the doctor talking about? Because, really, I'd always been robust and no one except Eliodoro de Cramentino, an Italian writer and disciple of Lombroso, Max Nordau and Pompeyo Gener, had thought of calling me a "degenerate masochist to the highest degree," due to my novel about the carnal mysteries of Parisian occultism.

"But do you really think I'm ill?" I asked him.

"Without a doubt, and if you'd like to know of what, I'll tell you of everything, or almost everything: of the intellect, the nerves and the will, of what is most interesting, in short, and most grave."

The reply of the wise old man made me think of my poor friend Marcelo, mystic poet of the *Hateful Rhymes*, who'd written an entire book trying to prove that all those who didn't think as he did were madmen or ill.

"The unfortunate thing, Doctor, is that for the ills you note in my organism, no pharmacist sells remedies and no doctor gives prescriptions."

"You're mistaken, sir. Today the study of such ailments, which twenty years ago were classified as 'characteristic signs of temperament', is more advanced than the knowledge of certain illnesses as ancient as typhoid fever and Asian cholera. From Charcot to the current day, we've traveled far, far, far; and after working patiently, amidst the indifference of the public in general and the malicious jibes of unimaginative professors in particular, we've at last managed to establish on solid ground, on experimental foundations, the most interesting of modern sciences: the science of ideological and sensitive illnesses . . . Fever is unpleasant and dangerous—who doubts it?—consumption is also dangerous and unpleasant, no one denies it; but the consumptives and feverish know how to live with it, of course, they know their maladies and can try to cure themselves with commonly available pills and traditional methods of hygiene, while poor men who, like you, seem healthy yet sustain psychic ills, suffer and die, usually without realizing that they carry in the depths of their degenerate beings a true moral cancer . . . If you knew how numerous, in the world of art and thought, are those who suffer almost without knowing it! . . . In the past month over a hundred of your colleagues came to my clinic of psychopathy . . . poor boys! . . . You should come too, and come soon; your illness must still not be very deeply rooted . . . what's more, the medicines are so pleasant, almost only healthy readings, trainings in aesthetic and moral reaction, ventures that work in a way that reflects in the nervous system . . . come . . ."

One morning I went to the clinic where the doctor was carrying out his role as spiritual analyst and psychological healer. I went out of pure curiosity, as someone who's not superstitious goes to hear what a palm reader has to say.

The first thing that called my attention, on finding myself in the "Clinic," was the almost stingy modesty of the room: in the back was a sofa; next to it was a table covered in books; then there were a few chairs, nothing else.

When I arrived, almost all the chairs were already occupied by people awaiting their turn.

"Number five!" said the doctor in a loud voice.

A gentleman occupying the first seat stood up and went to sit by the old wise man, to explain the symptoms of his occult illness:

"I, sir," he said, "am a painter; I'm thirty years old and have never spent a day in bed, but for some time now . . ."

"Lower your voice," the doctor ordered.

For a few minutes all that was heard in the vast dismantled room was the incomprehensible murmur of the sick man as he talked, and the dry impatient coughs of those waiting.

I looked at the doctor and almost didn't recognize him. He seemed to me transfigured by magic art. Now he wasn't the old man who often came to drink his aperitif in the café on Rue François I. Through thick glasses, his eyes shone in a peculiar way; his forehead of parchment was vaster; his hands moved nervously in an almost

feverish rhythm; his head of white hair tipped forward
had metallic gleams and youthful waves; his whole being,
in short, vibrated and trembled.

When "number five" had finished talking, the wise
man said to him:

"That's enough, Mr. Coriolis. Tomorrow you will receive my first instructions."

Coriolis? . . . Where had I seen that name written? . . .
Ah! yes, in the catalogs of the great painting exhibitions
and the booklets of art criticism . . . But how could that
be the famous Coriolis, the famous artist, the colorist
whose paintings full of sun and fertile life had dazzled
the members of the Institute?

III

"Number twelve!"

No one answered.

"Number twelve!"

The gentleman sitting by my side let me know that
"number twelve" was me.

When he recognized me, the doctor stood up.

"Come," he said, and led me to a neighboring room
in which there was no furniture.

When we were alone, he stretched out his hand with
true warmth, and thanked me.

"But why such gratitude?"

"For having come, sir, nothing else but for having
come. You are one of the cases I imagine will be most
interesting; you represent, for me, the most intense inner
illness in the most complete exterior robustness; you will

be one of my favorite 'cases'. But unfortunately you have come late and now we don't have time to speak seriously, so we'll leave the consultation for tomorrow. What do you think of my clinic?"

"It seems very curious to me, above all because of those who frequent it; all are people of distinguished appearance, and none have the face of an ill person . . . By the way, who is that Coriolis of 'number five'? I don't suppose it could be the young painter, the rival of Decamps."

"That's him, precisely."

"And he's ill?"

"Almost as much as you are; you need only see his works to understand it; his cerebral titillation is sharp and profound, and obliges him to look for nuances that don't exist in nature, to attempt to discover invisible details, to combine his colors in a way that produces implausible reflections. Haven't you seen his great canvas of '97? Those prisms of filtered light and that complicated spectrum of strong tones on pale ones would be enough to claim that the author is gravely ill from titillation, from 'supreme vice' as the graphomaniac Péladan would say. And, furthermore, this ill is complicated in him by ideological satyriasis, as is indicated by the naked body, covered in bubbles of soap, of his main figure beside the body of a black woman, also naked and painted with loving and painful enthusiasm. Amongst my clients, only Durtal[1] presents a case of erotic titillation as serious as that which I believe to exist in Coriolis."

---

1 The protagonist of four novels by J.-K. Huysmans, who was in fact a thinly disguised version of the author.

"But, is Durtal ill too?; Durtal, the historian and artist, the admirable author of the *History of Gilles de Rais* and *Occultism in the Middle Ages?*"

"Him too! . . ."

IV

The professional revelations of the doctor began to interest, worry, unsettle me.

That Coriolis was ill and trying to change his way of feeling, I could let slip; but that Durtal, the only erudite artist of my period, my dear and admirable master Durtal whose style and philosophy were, for me, literary sacraments, believed himself to be unhealthy in spirit and turned to Larriviere for a cure, seemed to me a sacrilege, almost an intellectual crime.

The doctor went on:

". . . Yes, Durtal too . . . and not just in any way, but gravely. All his works are true productions of a maniac and degenerate. In each page written by him, one sees without difficulty the hesitating weakness of the intellect, the desire to take pleasure in an object without the awareness that it is satisfying an insatiable thirst for diabolic, arrogant and obscene fantasies. Take a look at his lascivious images and read immediately afterward the most risqué tales of the abbé of Boissenon . . . what a visible difference! What Durtal says today is, no doubt, less indecent than what the great libertine vicar said a century ago; yet how great is the moral distance that separates the storyteller of the eighteenth century from our contemporary! The first wrote after eating; he wrote happily, like one telling a fresh anecdote, without tormenting himself, without looking for complicated means to give perfume and color to his phrase: his tales are 'healthy' and almost not immoral in the true sense of the word, since they make you laugh and present Vice from its comic side. Not so the pretentious descriptions of the chronicler of *Gilles de Rais*, who searches in the written word for illegitimate tones full of agonizing languishings and supernatural passions . . ."

V

Then the doctor spoke to me of Claude Larcher[1] and Charles Demailly,[2] two exquisite novelists, friends of mine, who had written some enchanting books on modern love.

"The two are ill," Larriviere told me, "since they suffer from severe graphomania. Demailly, above all, grieves me seriously due to his sentimental character and nervous irritation. Larcher is, at least, what one calls a 'smiling' or 'spiritual' man, who lets himself be carried away by the desire to startle and who, instead of dominating the phrase, yields to the demands of composition and style. I am sure that between Larcher and Demailly there is a great difference . . ."

---

1 The supposed author of Physiologie de l'amour moderne (1890) by Paul Bourget.
2 The protagonist of the Goncourt brothers' novel of the same name, describing the life of a man of letters.

VI

A gentleman opened the door of the room and came to greet us.

"Wait for me in the clinic," the doctor said.

Then, looking at me fixedly:

"Did you see that young man?" he asked.

"Who is it?"

"René Vincy."

"The author of *Sigisbeo*, the poet who was almost great in his first work, who tried to commit suicide and who now writes ridiculous novels worthy of George Ohnet?"

"The very one . . . only his novels are very honorable . . . He is the oldest of my patrons . . . he is my pride . . . Do you remember the circumstances of his suicide attempt? Well: as I was then the doctor of his family, they called me, and I saved him physically, and later on also intellectually and morally . . . Poor boy! His friend Larcher had filled his brain with madness. I threw all his manuscripts into the fire, and during his convalescence did not permit him to read anything but healthy books, the works of Laviche, Sarcey, George Sand; then I advised him to write balanced novels. And there you have it: thanks to my regime, his is now a man of letters worthy of competing with the author of *Serge Panine* . . . But we have already talked for too long, and it is necessary for me to leave you. Goodbye, see you later . . . see you tomorrow . . . tomorrow we will begin."

VI

"See you tomorrow," I said.

Naturally, I never went back. Why would I have returned? For him to cure me, converting my madness into idiocy? No, I have already made my definite decision; and given that in the world of letters it is necessary to choose between Bourgeoisie and Illness, I'll stick with Illness.

The Colonel's Tragedy

For Mariano de Cavia

I

THE colonel read the letter he'd just received; he read and reread it, almost without understanding it.

Could it be for him?

". . . My dear Julio: There's no doubt that you are a lion and an eagle eye. In the barracks nothing escapes your vigilance, not a button too few on the coat of a soldier, or a patch too many on the trousers of a sergeant, or even the poorly sewn-on buckle of some suspenders. Truly, you are a great eagle eye. You are also a lion, since in Crimea you shaved in front of the enemy . . ."

"Necessarily," he said to himself, "this letter is for me, since no one else but me had the youthful braggadocio to trim his beard under a rain of Russian bullets . . . But the rest . . ." And he went on reading:

". . . But from Crimea to your house there's a great distance. In the heart of your family you are neither a lion nor an eagle eye, my dear Julio. Do you know why?

No; you must not know, you cannot know, you do not know. If you knew, you would have already kicked out both of them, her and him. Because this is just it: a very vulgar matter of female and male; a little matter of love, one of those intrigues that occur in many honest situations without anyone noticing, but that when they happen in the home of the squadron chief make the soldiers and neighbors smile. Open your eyes, then, my terrible Julio, and if you do not want your troops to continue poking fun at your vigilance, pay attention to your adjutant, prepare the tip of your boot to give a good kick, and be careful."

No signature.

II

Who could have written this hotchpotch of lies? Perhaps an unhappy official, or a nasty joker, or an enemy without scruples.

But what if it were true?

He began to shout for his wife:

"Julia, Julia, come right away, Julia!"

He was prepared to question her meticulously, to discover the truth at all costs, to teach her a lesson if necessary.

While his wife was coming, he read the letter again, for the fifth or sixth time: "Pay attention to your adjutant, prepare the tip of your boot to give a good kick, and be careful."

The informer was right: above all it was necessary to be very careful and to transform himself into a spy, before becoming an accuser and executioner.

"Let us be clever," he thought, "and after that we will be terrible. A boot? As if that were enough! A couple of pistols, two bullets, one for her and the other for him . . ."

III

He called his adjutant:

"Tonight," he told him, "I am obliged to eat away from home and certainly will not return before twelve or one. You can do what you like, so long as you do not miss the review tomorrow. The night is yours, go now."

Then he made as if to leave and silently shut himself away in his room, prepared to observe what would happen in his house during his feigned absence.

IV

. . . In those hours of anxiety and rage, his whole past life passed before his memory. He remembered his mother, a good lady from a different time, devoted, uneducated and simple—she certainly would not have been capable of lying, deceiving, degrading the name of her husband! The king himself would have found her unyielding in her garb of candor and chastity: "Poor mother! . . ." He remembered the school where he had learned to read and pray . . . he remembered his friends from childhood—what had they all gone on to do?—and his first girlfriend—where was she now?—All his miseries and previous sufferings now seemed to him bearable, almost sweet, in comparison with his current tragedy. He would have given half his life to once again find himself in the carriage of the ambulance that had picked him up, dying, his skull cracked and his leg broken, after the battle in the Crimea.

Every few minutes a profanity slipped from his lips:

"It is necessary to kill them," he said to himself, "it is necessary to kill them . . . Honor before all else . . . Laugh at myself and have people point their finger at me? Isn't it necessary to do much more? Christ himself would divide them in four pieces to give to the dogs . . . And they say that blood stains! No, blood does not stain . . . blood purifies . . . it is necessary to bathe myself in blood and present myself thus, with hands red, and uniform red, and feet red, so that those who now make fun of me, recognize me, and so that the world, the whole world, everyone, is frightened . . . and so they know honor is honor and there is nothing greater than honor!"

His fists clenched the keys to the desk in spasms of rage, until the physical suffering was unbearable.

V

Then came the moments of humble sadness. To kill a soldier in war or kill a man in a duel would be perfectly justifiable; but to kill thus, in darkness, a woman, one's own, the partner of his existence, who had been poor

54

with him, the mother of his children! . . . To dishonor Federico so that his classmates at school turned their backs on him! . . . To leave Helena an orphan at fifteen years old, when she was so pretty and sensible! . . . What right did he have, as killer of their mother, to kiss his children? They would be horrified with him . . . . But it was necessary, it was fatally necessary.

"My God! My God!"

And seeing no way out, the poor soldier without beliefs fell to weeping, and tried to speak with the Virgin: "Saint Mary, Mother of Mercy, Our Lady . . ." By a miracle he did not understand, the prayers of his childhood, forgotten for thirty years, flowed complete from his lips, without any alteration, with all the naïve freshness of their ardent phrases.

VI

After much despair and many tears, the colonel tried to overcome his own desperation and prepare a plan.

In the first place it was necessary to kill the guilty ones; in this there was no room for any reasoning.

Then, so as not to be witness and victim to the pain of his children, it would also be necessary to kill himself.

"I will go afterward, and thus no one will be able to laugh in my beard or hold me in horror. My children may curse me if they like, but they will not do so in front of me, they will not distance themselves from me in terror, they will not be afraid of me."

He began to write his last will: "Dear children, children of my soul, little children of mine: Forgive, before anything else, the crime I have committed, which deprives you of the support of the only two beings who truly interested themselves in you. From today it will be necessary for you to continue alone on the path of life, without guidance and without support. The hand of your mother will be unable to caress you; the arm of your father will be unable to defend you. Do not ever forget me, and try to behave, during all the circumstances of existence, as if I were by your side. Do not forget her either, nor curse her, for if she was a criminal in a moment of madness, before this she was the best of mothers. God himself will forgive her, because God always forgives. I do not; I cannot; as I also cannot continue to live by your side; I cannot! The only thing I leave you is a name stained in blood: do not abandon it, do not change it for another; keep it as it is, for even full of shame, it must be sacred to you. Be honest; be strong; be loyal. That is all I ask of you and all I advise you. Later on there people will not be lacking who claim I was a bloodthirsty fool, and your mother a villainess; do not believe them; your mother was weak and criminal; I was a just man. Goodbye, goodbye."

The colonel read the lines he had just written and took a look to see if he had said all that he wanted to say. His moral testament seemed to him too harsh and too solemn. It was necessary to write it again in a different way, longer, more tender, with more advice and less pride.

He took up the pen a second time and began once more: "Little children of my heart, little children of mine: I write to you for the last time, in the most terrible circumstances of life, at one of those moments that men do not lie; I write to you with my soul, after having shed many tears and kissed your adored images; little children of mine . . ."

An almost imperceptible sound of hushed voices and stealthy footsteps made him stand up.

VII

With gun in hand, crawling so as not to be seen, holding his breath so as not to be heard, he emerged from his room.

The door of the entrance was half-open. In the depths of the hallway, beside the room of the housekeeper, a lamp gave out a pale gleam.

"I have a moment now," thought the colonel. "It is essential to recover my sangfroid, so as not to seem like a killer but a dispenser of justice."

And as if he were in the war, he mentally ordered:

"Forward!"

Yet none of his limbs moved.

"Am I afraid?" he continued to think. "Could I abandon my revenge? No, no. There they are, him, with his appearance of a musketeer, vain, handsome, stupid; and her, still beautiful, wearing out her last ardent kisses, far from me . . . And in the room of Irene, the maid! . . . So the maid knows everything and has already been able to tell the neighbors and doormen . . . and as an accomplice of my wife, she also threatens her, no doubt . . . But if they are occupying her bed, where is she, the maid? There too? . . . Watching everything? It is necessary to end this, finish it once and for all . . . Forgive me, my children . . . forgive me . . . Forward!"

<h2 style="text-align:center">VIII</h2>

. . . Already he had removed the safety and pressed his finger to the trigger of the gun, when a sharp voice gave a penetrating cry:

"Killer, killer, help!"

Killer? No; he was not a killer: he did not want to be taken for a killer; he was a judge, an executioner, a wild animal, everything, in short, but a killer.

He took a step backward.

"Come closer," he said to his adjutant, "and you will see if I am a killer; come look at me beside the lamp."

The official did not move.

"You won't come closer?" he went on. "You won't come closer? You don't want to defend yourself? Would you prefer me to kill you like a dog? Even better . . . coward!"

Then she, the woman in bed alongside the official, went to kneel before the colonel:

"Forgive me—sir—forgive me! Do not kill him, do not kill him!"

The one who spoke thus, pleading for mercy, was the maid. The colonel recognized her, he let the gun fall, he kneeled alongside her to see her up close, touch her, convince himself it was not an illusion; and with his cheeks covered in tears, smiling nervously, like a madman, like a maniac, like an idiot, he said to her: "Is it you? . . . Truly, is it you? Irene . . . Poor little one . . . You? You? . . . My good Irene? . . . Come closer . . . come . . . Yes; yes; talk to me . . . Tell me it's real, it's true . . . Irene! . . . my good Irene . . . my poor little one . . ."

Stories from the North

For D. Elias Zerolo

I have a friend named Yalor de Gontrant, a storyteller and poet, descendant of the ancient Dutch singers, who lives in Holland under the cold shadow of barbarian holm oaks and only leaves his country once a year to go south in search of sun and enthusiasm. On occasion he stops for a few days in Paris to tell us the stories and legends he has just gathered with the piety of a modern rhapsodist in the northern villages.

"You," he tells us, "live here amidst artificial phrases and refined ideas. It is necessary that the adventures of my little princesses, my ghosts, my warriors and nuns, make you understand that there is also beauty beyond elegant artifice."

. . . And thus, while he is among us, the literary evenings of the Latin Quarter always end with one of these small stories from the North, which are delicate and mysterious, and which, like opium, lead one to dream.

✳

One day it occurred to me to ask him if the legends he told us were new.

"Yes," he answered, "they are new in Paris where you are all ignorant and scornful; but in Belgium and Holland they are ancient. The youngest is one hundred years old, like the daughters of King Troldo. My friends and I take them from old books, give them a layer of varnish and add our signatures so that *L'Indépendance Belge*, the *Walonia* and the *Echo du Nord* pay us for them. As soon as I arrive back in my land, I will clip a few from my collections of newspapers by Daxhelat, Buscher, Severin, Khan, Brohan, Marrés and myself, to send to you."

Here are some of those legends:

I

The Palace of Rose Marble

Tilia and the Troubadour left the mansion that had been destroyed by the red soul of the Horseman and walked, holding hands, their feet bare, without speaking, like two poor children who are very afraid.

They walked along the plain for entire weeks; they walked for long months, they walked, they walked. And the plain, always red, always immense, stretched out before their tranquil eyes.

At last, one morning, they stopped at the edge of a lake whose water, clear and pale, made them think of a weave of moonbeams. The swans of snow and daydream moved their great wings with shudders of silver, swimming toward a rowboat of dull gold.

The Troubadour and Tilia climbed into the rowboat which began to slip, gently and as if by enchantment, into the water, without any oar disturbing the serenity of the lake.

*

At night the lovers became aware of a marvelous park whose trees, swayed by the languid air, produced the notes of a melancholic and ancient refrain.

On the beach was a mysterious lady, wrapped in a cloak of purple bespangled with gold stars.

The rowboat stopped alongside the lady.

The lady said:

"Children who adventure thus in the Sea of Chimera, tell me who you are and where you come from."

"We come," replied Tilia, "from the land of Campinia where the red soul of the Horseman has brought death to men and set fire to the villages. I am Queen Tilia and this is my Troubadour."

The lady continued to speak:

"You are perhaps the lovers of which legend speaks . . . I am also a queen . . . I am the devastated princess of the island of Thule. In my kingdom all the knights perished when my father threw the cup of Love from the battlement of his castle . . . Come and you will see my palace

of rose marble that has a hundred turrets of gold, and
the mysterious park that served as a bedchamber to the
King of Thule and the Queen of Bohemia . . . Come . . .
Under that enormous willow rest the remains of my father; under the other, those of my mother, who was more
beautiful than the dawn; the great knights are under that
holm oak . . . come."

✳

They entered the palace through three gates of ivory;
they climbed up three staircases of marble and arrived at
the turrets of gold.

The princess took a seat and said to the pensive
lovers:

"When I was young and beautiful, I had the cowardly
idea of saving the island of Thule by seducing the six
kings that lay siege to it . . ."

Then she told her tale:

"From a country in the East, there came to con-
quer Thule six kings who were very handsome, very rich
and very powerful, whose wide cloaks of silk rippled in
the mist. Before the citadel of a hundred turrets, they
planted their great swords, swearing by their six gods
that the king was going to die and that Thule was going
to lose its turrets as soon as the sun melted the mists.
At midnight the princess of Thule, wrapped in a veil of
moonlight, went to the camp of the enemy kings led by
the immaculate swan, in the mist of the dark night. The
princess kissed the eyes of the foreign kings six times and
caressed the six hateful foreheads . . . Since then, in the

islands of the songs, there have been only blind kings who walk through the forest, crying without shedding a tear . . .

"Yes, my father has condemned me to wander without rest, for a hundred years, on this island lacking in love . . . For, on this island, there is no love and all the creatures that arrive here must forever renounce caresses, kisses and desires. If your lips murmur: 'I love you', if your sighs sing: 'I worship you', the jealous soul of my father will awaken under the willow and go riding roughly over the hundred turrets of gold."

Tilia and the Troubadour were led mysteriously to the room of the tower where the king had sat with pride for many years, before he killed Love by throwing the cup of gold into the depths of the lake.

Both were sad.

After gazing at one another with eyes of anguish, they leaned on the railing of rose marble, and dreamed.

". . . Not to love . . . Then why did Night caress the lake with ardor? . . . Why did the silence sing sweet songs? . . . Why did the palace evoke, with the roses of its marble, the warm marble of human roses? . . . No doubt the august princess is mad . . . Isn't that right, Tilia? . . . Troubadour, isn't that right? . . ."

Their lips came together to respond with an ardent and devoted kiss.

The next day, when the princess entered the great tower, she saw her two guests turned into statues of rose marble.

II

. . . In this way, then, the pensive lovers fleeing from the country devastated by the red soul of the Horseman took refuge in the castle of the King of Thule, and paid for the ardor of their last kisses with eternal stillness. The story seems to me simple and pleasant. It also seems to me philosophical.

Upon passing through the modernist brains of the young Belgians, the Walloon and Dutch legends lose much of the archaic flavor of the old barbarian myths, but conversely acquire a certain refined vagueness which the primitive stories never had.

My good companion Gontrant has written, at the margin of each clipping, the period to which the legend corresponds. According to his notes, *The Palace of Rose Marble* is a medieval tale; then comes a sketch from the Renaissance, and afterward a little scene from the eighteenth century. Here they are:

The Bloody Flowers of the Apostle

When the women told their husbands that the man from the plain had the gift of prediction, many peasants went to ask him how the next harvest would be.

He replied to them by pointing to the fields where ample waves of wheat shivered:

"The sky is blue and the wind has calmed; but it doesn't matter; before a hundred hours have passed, the sky will turn black and without mercy the wind will uproot all your plants, dragging them along miserably amidst a storm of mud. And then you will cry, for you laughed when I wanted to cry."

Some days later, an icy and dirty hurricane did destroy the great sown fields.

The men without faith yelled, their hands clenched:

"This has been done by the man of the plain. Our women and children are going to die of hunger . . ."

The man returned to the city, and said:

"Come to me, I come on behalf of God, and bring you Truth and Joy and Health; come to me and I will tell you how, after death, your sorrows will be greater if you do not listen to me; I will give you the blessing and the key to heaven if you believe in Our Lord; come to me to learn, and console yourselves, and be good . . ."

The response of the town was a rain of stones and curses.

The man went back to the plain, sad and alone.

The chief of the city sent a troop of lancers a few days later, with the aim of asking the "madman" what would happen if the town persisted in not believing in God.

"If the people do not believe," he replied, "half the town will die so the other half can be saved."

The soldiers set his shack on fire and went away, roaring with laughter.

A day later the plague killed a hundred thousand people.

✳

Then the same cavalry returned to the countryside by order of the chief and seized the prophet to lead him to the palace of the city, where he was lashed and bound in chains.

During the night of that same day, the whole region trembled and half the houses collapsed, while seven men of good will went to request that they be bound in chains alongside the man from the plain.

The chief, not happy to agree to what they asked, ordered that a thousand lashings be given to each of them. All suffered the punishment without blinking and then kneeled to give thanks to God:

"There are seven of us," they said, "and the prophet will save us because we believe in him and in God."

"We will see," roared the chief and, calling to his lancers, ordered them to quarter the eight prisoners and afterward scatter their softened and throbbing limbs through the countryside.

So they did.

And for that reason, ever since then, the flowers of the Region of the Archers have always been red.

III

A Dream

Lying down in his noble bed, the adolescent tried to reconstruct the pale and intense vision of his last daydream of love.

It seemed to him he had been in a strangely adorned hall, amidst young marquises covered in old emblems and virgin princesses crowned in rose-colored flowers. All spoke of the subjects of the earth as of things that were old and distant. A pale woman, above all, told the others her story, in such a serene way that no one wondered about the horrible tortures to which she was referring.

All of a sudden a marquis stopped before the adolescent and exclaimed:

"Some were born to love; others to be loved." The men smiled; the women went pale.

What else, God of mine? . . . The adolescent saw the smiles, heard the sighs and lost himself in the vagueness of dream, when a precise vision appeared before his memory in the misty scenery of a small poorly lit garden.

. . . Blonde, yes, very blonde, the virgin went toward him; she went slowly for fear that two tears trembling on her eyelids would trickle down her cheeks. The shy adolescent went out to meet her. Notes of the orchestra came from the hall, and in the air floated an intense fragrance of rice powder and feminine wigs.

✳

Seated on a marble bench, beside the cold plinth of a faun, amidst the trees, the adolescent and the virgin contemplated one another, without speaking, almost without seeing each another, wrapped in the cloak of desires and hopes.

So an hour passed, until behind them a sound of kisses and sighs made them blush, the virgin, ah, so blonde! and the adolescent, oh, so shy! . . .

The powdered marquis stopped again before the adolescent and completed his sentence:

". . . others to be loved, but only those with virgin souls."

Then the lovers unclasped their hands and moved away, frightened, from the white plinth on which there smiled a faun of marble.

Marta and Hortensia

For Manuel Rodríguez Mendoza

WHEN dinner had ended, the man with green eyes pulled me away from the others and said:

"All those gentlemen talking just now with enthusiasm about the fidelity of their wives and the love of their dear ones are mere idiots, unless they are hypocrites. In Paris and all the great cities of the world, the ancient love, the true love that my poor friend Larcher called love-passion, no longer exists but as a rare case, the subject of a novel or the sign of psychological fragility.

"As for me, I am a weakling, a slow one, a survivor from older generations. I once believed in love as a religion. I was mad, yes, completely mad, for a woman who was worth neither more nor less than women in general . . . You must have known her: she is named Marta de San Lys, and at heart she is a monster; but since she had eyes that were very blue, very tender and very big, a head of hair that was very blonde, hands that were very aristocratic and very innocent lips, everyone took her for an angel. Marcelo Verdi, the poet of *Poisoned Violets*, often called her Our Lady of the Smile, and the old painter La Plane always advised her to wear white, all white, to look like the fragile and sickly madonnas from religious paintings of the Middle Ages.

"My God . . . How easy it is to blaspheme unconsciously! . . . I myself, who should have known her, kneeled every night before her to recite to her the litanies of my passion. 'Rose,' I said, 'virginal rose, hyacinth of flesh, lily of love, gate to goodness and joy, sacred altar, sealed cup, inexhaustible cup of pleasure, pious bird, blonde bird, incomparable dove, be mine, be mine forever!'

"And indeed for two years she was mine in appearance, always mine.

"Living by my side, letting herself be adored, lazily obeying my whims, dominating me in a clever way, falling asleep out of idleness in my arms, vegetating, in short, like an anemic plant in a greenhouse of luxury, she let me believe that God had heard my delirious vows and that her love was equal to mine.

"On certain occasions, however, seeing the crease of fatigue that gave to her lips an expression of infinite blessedness, I suffered, thinking that my caresses could be too violent for her flesh of silk, and that my breath of fire might hurt her blossom of a mouth. Thus, more than once I resolved to myself not to employ in our amorous games anything but refined methods, methods in the style of Louis XV, something that was at the same time courtesy and passion, essence of roses and pepper, humility and frenzy . . . Madness!"

✳

The man with green eyes rested his hands on the marble of the hearth, as if to refresh them, and then lifted them to his forehead.

He went on:

"Have you read the secret chronicles of the court of France? In one of them there is a very curious story, an anecdote worthy of Brantôme. It is the story of a gentleman who slept with the Infanta and went to his amorous meetings carrying a whip to provide his sweet royal beloved with the pleasure of brutality, which, it appears, is one of the pleasures that ladies best know how to savor. At times I imagine that if instead of buying bunches of violets I had bought a cat-o'-nine-tails . . .

"But no . . . that would also have been useless. Marta had, in her blood and her nerves—in her nerves especially—the same illness as almost all the Parisian ladies of her time. Marta was not born for man. Don Juan would have made her laugh with his old-fashioned kisses, and the duke of Richelieu would only have managed to call her attention thanks to his diamonds.

"I do not believe she ever, not during her walks, not at her dances, turned her head to pay attention to a man; no, never! Women, on the other hand, attracted her, seduced her, drove her mad.

"At first she took the trouble of looking for a thousand excuses to admire those who passed by our side or begin talking with those who ate at our same restaurant table. 'Look at that dress,' she said to me, 'look at it closely.' And while I looked at an unremarkable *toilette*, she devoured with her eyes of a primitive virgin, with her eyes divinely blue, what was within the dress.

"Later on, her admiration came to be open, almost shameless. Her girlfriends were everything to her.

"Her girlfriends, did I say? No, her girlfriend; because Marta never had but one girlfriend, only one, who lasted a month, or a week, or an hour, and later disappeared from our life, to leave the place to another. Thus, during the two years of our common existence, there passed through the house more than thirty, more than forty women, all young, all pretty, always looking like Marta's sisters.

"And I lived uneasily in that perpetual movement of light dresses, delicate bodies and great heads of hair, imagining that my beloved one sought a sister of the soul in the world, and that her feminine inconstancy was nothing but the natural result of the selection all of us make in trying to find a true friend.

"So much did the spectacle of that instability come to grieve me that one day, one of those days a man is capable of everything to please the woman he loves, I decided to test a supreme idea: 'Marta,' I said to myself, 'is my wife before God, and if she is not before men, it is because she does not want it so. Marta forms part of my family; Marta is half of myself; my sister is her sister.'

"When in the depth of my brain I had pronounced this last phrase, all the tranquility in my life disappeared forever. I had wanted Marta to meet my sister Hortensia and be her friend. More than once I was on the point of making what are called introductions; but in the interior of my being there was something that opposed such friendship. Traditional worries, respect for family, vulgar contempt for the woman who is not our legitimate wife? . . . Perhaps.

"The light dresses kept coming and going before my eyes, without ever leaving in our nest an impression of lasting intimacy. And each day I desired with more ardor to see a single dress, to know that Marta was speaking to just one woman, to find her always by her side, to always see the same hat and same face, to put an end, at last, to that whirlwind of pretty figures that came, passed by, smiled and vanished in less than an instant.

"Yet, I did not dare to call my sister.

"I wish that I had never dared! But one afternoon, when a blonde head of hair had just vanished over our threshold, Marta said to me, or rather, to herself: 'They're all the same; they're all false!' I couldn't take it anymore: I took a carriage, and half an hour later my sister Hortensia entered into my bachelor's house, six months after having left the convent.

"After that, no woman came to visit us again. Marta seemed enchanted, Hortensia too.

"For a few months my joy would have been complete, were it not for those friends at the club who knew of the friendship that united Marta and Hortensia, and asked ironically after the 'two sisters'. I did not put great stock in those malicious indiscretions, and with my eyes sweetly half-closed, I lulled myself to sleep in the shadows of love and affection.

"Nevertheless, the day of the supreme disillusion arrived at last . . . Can't you guess what my supreme disillusion was . . . ?"

The man with the green eyes began to guffaw with laughter, moving his lips feverishly.

"Can't you guess . . . ?"

I thought his story was going to end in a grotesque way, and that the epilogue would be one of those comic scenes that represent two intimate friends pulling out their eyes over a hat's decoration or a rivalry in elegance.

"You'll see," concluded my interlocutor, "you will see . . . One night, coming home earlier than usual and believing that Hortensia had already left, I walked through the dining room in the darkness, arrived in the hall and was preparing to open the door that gave access to our bedroom, when a murmur of muffled voices froze the blood in my veins. The voice of my beloved spoke a thousand sweet words, a thousand passionate phrases . . . and I heard them, without being able to move . . . With whom was she speaking? What criminal and mysterious man was asking her to swear eternal fidelity and eternal love? . . . 'Tell me you will never forget me, tell me never . . . never . . . swear it to me! . . .' Yes, it was Marta who was requesting eternal promises . . . 'I swear to you!' replied the other voice, even more known and familiar to me than the first . . . My emotion was straight brandy, so intense was my rage that I couldn't even grab the handle of the door to the bedroom . . . After all, why open it if I've never been able to kill two women? . . ."

Ideal Love

I

12 July

GABRIEL has just left. He's a good boy, Gabriel . . .
Three years ago, when we saw each other for the
first few times, the only thing in him that I liked was his
way of mocking others seriously, severely, in an almost
priestly manner.

"That lady," he would often say to me, "is like the
moon."

Or else:

"That gentleman looks like a Brazilian count."

His jokes, lapidary and cruel, did not make me
laugh immediately, but they engraved themselves on my
memory and obsessed me to the point that three or four
days later, finding myself again before the lunar lady or
nouveau riche gentleman, it was almost impossible for me
not to burst into laughter.

Yet others have made any number of trivial and nasty
remarks, that are funnier no doubt, but have left no impression on my soul.

Could it be because the voice of Gabriel was sharper, more strident, more macabre? Could it be due to his attitude of a cold and impeccable dandy? Could it be? . . .

No; no . . . at that time I did not see him with tender eyes, I did not even pay any more attention to his figure than to those of the other "sportsmen" who tried to be pleasant to me.

Gabriel was not pleasant to me; just the opposite, he seemed to me disconcerting.

Why? . . .

II

13 July

Today, after having spent the morning in the company of Gabriel, I ask myself again why he interests me more than the rest.

Gabriel is not handsome, not by a long shot. His nose is too big; his head has begun to grow more barren of hairs than Apollo's; his beard is neither blond, nor black, nor curly, but is the poor beard of a studious man, one of those beards without color and without elegance, like that of Jules Lemaître or Brunetière; his body is less lithe and less flexible than that of any bicyclist.

Really, there is nothing more vulgar than his exterior aspect.

The only thing about him that seems to me beautiful, truly, completely, delicately and exquisitely beautiful, are his hands—those hands that are aristocratic and nervous, white like those of Whistler's princess, and so long, so tapered, so harmonious, that they could have served as a model for the sculptor Rodin, to complete the incorporeal beauty of his John the Baptist in bronze!

More than once, feeling my hand between his ideal hands at the moment for farewells, I have come to lose my habitual indifference, to indicate to him in an imperious manner that I would like to stay this way for a few moments more; that my hands desire to be caressed at length by his hands; that there is something, in the depth of my heart or depth of my mind, that feels itself swayed, weakened, tamed, during the ten seconds that our goodbyes last. But he has not wanted or has not known how to understand me. His "good afternoon" and his "goodbye" are always of a mathematical brevity.

III

17 July

For the last four days I've done nothing but think of the hands of Gabriel.

If Mama knew the preoccupied hours that I have passed trying to devise a discreet method to embrace those hands, I am sure she would mock me. But though Gabriel is my boyfriend, and though everyone lets us speak alone in the perfumed corners of the drawing room, to this day he has not even remarked to me on my black eyes.

How, then, do I know that he loves me?

Because women always know these things before anyone tells them.

And what's more, because my poor mother has told me so.

Apparently, Gabriel came to the house one Sunday last month, when I had gone to eat in the company of the marchionesses of Lorient, and asked permission from my family to court me. My family naturally granted permission and Mama told me about this act. I thought that the next day Gabriel would say something to me, but nothing, not a word, not a compliment; not even one of those smiles all men have at their disposal when they find themselves before a pretty woman.

Still, I am sure that he loves me . . . that he loves me a lot . . . that he adores me.

Today, when I put into practice the strategy that I invented to embrace his hand, I convinced myself that his love is as great as the greatest and as ardent as the most grand.

The bad thing is that what is felt thus cannot be explained in any way.

If someone were to *hear me think* and asked me about the signs that indicate my boyfriend's passion, it would put me in a very tight spot. Bourget himself, in collaboration with Marcel Prévost, wrote a hundred pages without being able to explain the thousand little things that indicate, in a shy, cold and proud soul like the soul of Gabriel, true passion.

The majority believe that men declare the love they feel through their gaze. I, for my part, believe the opposite. The man who can look directly at a woman does not truly love her. The man in love, the man who makes love a religion, lowers his eyes before the eyes of his idol; and when he focuses on her, when his pupils fix from afar through space on the ideal face, it is always feverishly, in a terrifying way, as if he has committed a crime. The man in love who feels surprised, in the act of mute adoration, by the object itself of that adoration, trembles and lowers his eyes.

Gabriel lowers his eyes when mine fix on him.

. . . If Luisa, my classmate from school, had seen me this morning! . . .

Because "strategies" are always bad. Our history teacher often told us that "Bismarck was the blond monster who received from hell the gift of the bloodthirsty strategy."

Thank God that mine has nothing bloodthirsty about it. Here it is: my granny, the good one, Papa's mother, gave me some time ago, on my saint's day, a ring: a very ugly ring, with an emerald, a ruby and a sapphire, something like the start of a rainbow, a kind of mélange of fake jewels. I'd wanted to throw it out the window, but Papa ordered me to put it on my finger so as not to upset the "old lady". Papa is an old military man: all women over twenty are old for him. So I put on the ring, resolving to lose it as quickly as possible; but as bad luck would have it, no one was able to remove it from my index finger.

All my friends have tried to remove it . . . Impossible, impossible . . .

The ring remains here, on my poor finger, not wanting to pass over the joint. Yesterday, after Gabriel told me about his last trip to Switzerland, I begged him to help me to separate myself from such a hateful jewel.

"Hateful!" he replied. "To my taste it is very pretty."

"Maybe, but it disgusts me."

"In that case it is necessary to remove it."

"I can't do it alone; will you help?"

"Me?"

"Yes, Gabriel, you must be more skilled than my friends."

And turning red like a poppy, with his eyes lowered and his lips dry, without saying a word, almost trembling, Gabriel, my poor Gabriel who is always so serious even when he mocks the rest, began to try to remove the ring. Naturally, he did not manage it. But that does not matter. What I desired was to have my hand between his for a few minutes.

IV

21 July

Truly I am in love with the hands of Gabriel. Each day I find in them a new charm, new beauty, new grace.

Sometimes they seem to me the hands of a wax statue, pale and almost supernatural. At other times, on the contrary, I seem to see in their movements something terrible, something that makes think of the claws of the great felines and birds of prey. They are cruel and gentle, inscrutable and soft, tyrannical and pleading.

They are fantastic . . . When they come together before the altar of the Virgin to pray, they call to mind the hands of the Christian martyrs made from the "flesh of the host," as Sister María de Agreda puts it.

When they shake in anger, they cannot help but look like the living evocations of those limbs that, in the stories of Edgar Poe and Hoffman, fabricate the ropes of those hanged in a dream . . .

V

22 July

I need to tell someone about the "disturbing" impressions the hands of my boyfriend produce in me. I need to find a confidant for my passionate secrets. I need somebody, anybody, to explain to me the mystery of my love . . .

But who? . . . Luisa? No; Luisa does not know Gabriel. Neither do the marchionesses of Lorient . . . So? . . . Mama? . . . Yes, Mama is the only one who can tell me the real truth, the only one who can give me good advice . . . She is so good, Mama.

VI

At last I have come to a decision. Today I told Mama the extraordinary sensation that the hands of Gabriel produce on my spirits.

She listened kindly, then said to me:

"The reason is very simple: Gabriel's hands please you because the hand is the symbol of pure love. To give the hand is to give the soul."

Innocent Mama! . . .

Nostalgia for Pain

I

WHEN he found himself an orphan, rich and free, the viscount thought what all men think at twenty-five years of age.

He thought of love. He thought of forming a family of his own choice, a family that was entirely his own, one of those families composed of only a man and a woman, that nonetheless are an entire universe . . . A woman! . . . A woman! . . .

The viscount could not conceive of life without a woman.—And during the first three months of his orphanhood, all his thoughts and calculations were dreams of love.

II

The most urgent thing was to build himself a mysterious and coquettish nest, a palace that made one think of the tiny trianon hats of eighteenth-century ladies, something at once rustic and refined, with loads of silk and many carpets inside, many trees outside, and amidst the trees many white statues, and added to that an infinity of discreet paths, some flowery grottos, a pond covered with swans from the North and Venetian gondolas . . .

III

The viscount was one of those shy and violent beings who take refuge in sentimentalism out of a hatred for the vulgar existence of our Century, and who go from hope to hope borne by a Chimera, preparing meticulously and mathematically the fulfillment of their singular desires without ever daring to go past preparations. Reality frightened him. The hypocritical and cunning battle of social life always found him prepared to let himself be defeated without resistance. He understood nothing but ancient times, the Franks, the noble and epic battles spoken of in the romantic poems of Victor Hugo and chivalrous novels of Alexandre Dumas.

His true vocation was war, not the modern war waged by avarice, ordered like a game of chess and composed of algebraic problems, but the war of Louis XIV, valiant and courtly, heroic and gallant, full of picturesque and cruel adventures without brutality.

How many times in his hours of vain fever had he not seen himself dressed in silk and lace, at the head of a column of gentleman soldiers, the tricorn hat in his right hand, saying to his troops a moment before setting forth: "Men, we are going to have the honor of a battle!" . . . How many times had his delirious dreams made him victoriously enter an enemy city following a pitched battle, under a rain of roses and laurels! . . . He would have set fire to buildings, he would have killed, he would have been heroic, bloodthirsty and magnanimous, if that would merit a smile, a wreath, applause!

But he had been born too late, and thought he saw only one refuge that provided an escape from the hateful democratic life of his century.—That refuge was Sentiment.

IV

Why, after having desired with such ardor a sweet and sensitive companion to complete the joy of his freedom and wealth, had he united with that devilish Loulou from the comic opera of the Bufos Parisienses, whose big eyes, a pale blue, almost white, seemed two lakes in which the souls of many poets had drowned?

Not even he knew exactly.—Perhaps it was the fault of Fate . . .

One night, leaving the theater, the viscount had led everyone to his Trianon to inaugurate the banquet hall.

During dinner, the drinks were served by Mauricio Noél, a journalist who had the specialty of wisely mixing five different wines in each cup, "with the object," according to him, "of being no less than Des Esseintes."

At the end of dinner, everyone stood up. It was four in the morning. Each woman looked for the arm of a man with a feline and automatic movement, shaking her head as if to remember something. Then the couples began to leave, moving slowly, almost mute, their faces pale, not leaving behind them anything but an echo of exhausted kisses and nervous laughter . . .

Only Loulou remained seated in her place.

"This morning," she said, "I am not leaving!"

Indeed, she did not leave that morning . . . nor the next day. And a month later, she and the viscount had still not left the perfumed refuge in whose pool there were swans from the North and Venetian gondolas.

V

The torments of the viscount increased at each moment. They were monotonous, ridiculous torments, full of humiliations; nervous torments that relaxed all the energetic fibers of his temperament; torments of jealousy, torments that make others laugh and sometimes have the power to kill.

Loulou was not harsh, or vulgar, or rough. She was cruel. When she came near the bed of her lover, she always carried a smile full of promises on her lips. When they went out together, all her affectionate gazes were for her master. To reproach her would have been to expose oneself as acting in one of those comedies in which the judge must ask for pardon from the accused.—Thus the viscount fled from any opportunity favorable to explanation, and continued to suffer, in silence, the miserable sorrows of his love and jealousy.

87

If only he had been able to find himself before a rival! If only one of those friends, who were never lacking, had given him real proof! . . . But no; there was no material proof. All was supposition, glances intercepted at the theater, rapid gestures half-glimpsed in the garden, nothing serious, in short. Yet he was sure it was true, that everyone was mocking him, that his beloved . . .

But what could he do to throw her in the street with honor? Because for the viscount, who still had some drops of feudal blood in his veins, forgiveness did not exist. Those who on a night of drunkenness swore friendship and later called him "sir" seemed to him unworthy of shaking his hand. Those who in an hour of madness offered him eternal love and later smiled while greeting another were for him "perjuring monsters."—His vocabulary had the same age as his soul: a thousand years.

VI

The only thing that arrived every so often to bring a rose-colored tint to his poor gray life were the letters from his uncle, the marshal, Laura's father.

Laura de Montigny!—The name evoked in the viscount's brain a whole universe of sweet friendship, tranquil affection, chaste love. If only he had married her! . . . If only he had known! . . . If only he could!

And every month, when the letter arrived, Loulou's lover could not fall asleep without dreaming of the joy of having a true family and the happiness of not suffering, not doubting, not despising the one who lived by his side . . .

But the problem of leaving his beloved did not have, for him, any solution.

At last Loulou herself resolved it without anyone advising her, leaving in the company of a traveling comedian who was going to seek his fortune in America.

VII

A month later, the viscount and his cousin married . . . And on the day of the wedding, returning from the church, while the bride, dressed in white, smiling and simple, looked with admiration at her rural and refined nest, the viscount, whose soul had been made to suffer, understood that he had just lost his only source of activity, the activity of his sentimental restlessness, and that from this moment on, the tranquil existence of the true family would be for him as empty, as solitary, as icy, as the bed in which Loulou had slept for the last time . . .

Restless Soul

For Clarín

I

I don't think that I've ever been a child; I have never lived in the countryside; and yet, this morning, when I woke up in the monk's bed of my cell facing a window full of flowers, I thought that I experienced a childlike sensation. Where had I seen, at dawn, a narrow and flowery window like my religious balcony? Nowhere. When had I passed a night in the countryside? Never.

No; never.—Just like almost all Parisians, my compatriots, I was born already aged in the tiny room of a dark house; I spent my first years between the walls of a school, never saw anything but the almost artificial trees of the Bois du Boulogne, and never found myself outside the fortifications after twelve at night.

The only country sunrises I can remember are those about which I have read, those that books have made appear before my vision, sunrises seen by others, in short.

And even so, my artificial impressions have come to confuse themselves in such a way with my real impressions that my first idea, upon opening my eyes today, was an idea of memory. I believed myself to have contemplated those flowers and that great light-filled space in another time, in my childhood, in the true spring of life . . .

Now I laugh at myself and my lack of sincerity with my own soul; yet the truth is that the fault isn't mine, but that of the novelists who continue to make us see the eternal scene of childhood in a landscape of flowers and pure air. If someone speaks to us of a very happy child, we naturally imagine him to ourselves in the back yard of a farm . . . There is nothing that falsifies our impressions so much as literature.

At nine in the morning the chaplain came to visit with the aim of precisely knowing my mood. It appears that the superior had recommended him to treat me with great caution. His first question was so modest and so simple it almost seemed to me ridiculous:

"Are you a philosopher?"

"No, Father, I am not; if I were I would not be here, in search of Consolation and Oblivion. I do not have to repent for any immense sin: my life has been neither worse nor better than that of almost anyone else; but I have loved much and suffered much; and as in Paris it is ridiculous to cry, and as to cry alone is horrible; and as I do not expect anything, or desire anything; and as she deceived me, I came to believe that the best refuge was here . . . More than to be converted, I have come to cry, to hide away, to avoid seeing others laugh."

His definitive advice made me lose a great part of the faith I have always had in the talent of the confessors in monasteries.

"To leave our soul in the hands of a woman," he told me, "would be like setting out in a broken skiff; the only one who can give us joy is Our Lady."

. . . I think that if my doorwoman had been Catholic, she would have told me the same thing.

II

Could it be through a work of divine power? Could it be due to the strangeness that everything has for me here? Could it be an effect of fatigue? The fact is that during the three days I have spent in the monastery, I almost haven't suffered.

"I almost haven't suffered!" Here is a phrase that I never imagined I could write again.

I think that I am beginning to be cured. Today I have undergone a truly cruel experience: I have remained alone with my memories and have made my Soul contemplate all the circumstances of its Pain . . . My joyful life, my fanatical love for Luisa, the first two years of our union, her caresses, my blind confidence in her and her affection, all that could prepare my Soul for the tragedy to seem horrific to it, in short, I have reviewed slowly, coldly, cruelly. I have spoken to it of betrayal, I have spoken to it the name of the other, I have repeated to it the detailed and ridiculous circumstances of the abandonment, I have assured it that many, in my case, have the right to kill or die; I have reminded it of the expression of a thousand unforgettable smiles, a thousand mysterious gazes . . . And yet, my poor withered and ill Soul has suffered before the complete horror of the scene less than what it suffered a week ago at the shadow of an unremarkable detail.

Praised be to God who is beginning to have pity on me!

III

My good chaplain has given me a copy of *The Imitation of Christ*.

I have never much liked this authoritarian book, dry and paradoxical, and now that I have read it for the third or fourth time, at the moment when I have most felt the necessity of moral relief, my small sympathy has turned into true resentment against the friar who wrote it. No doubt poor Kempis isn't to blame that critics have considered his meditation to be an inexhaustible fount of moral consolations, but truly I think that to give the *Imitation* to a man who suffers is to deceive and mock him. May God forgive me if I blaspheme. Amidst all the solemn and somewhat pretentious maxims of the famous book, there is not a single one that is truly human. "Distance yourself from the world, since the further you are from the world, the closer you are to heaven." "Despise temptations, which are only images of sin . . ." Yes, all this is excellent, but it doesn't give us the slightest indication of the means we must use to distance ourselves from the world or escape from temptation. And then, how little ardor there is in the phrases! What a lack of exaltation, lyricism, poetry! For me the only books that have a true religious influence on tormented souls are the ardent and mad mystical treatises of Saint Teresa and Sister Emmerich, in which there is no rhetoric of any kind, and which are simple, supernatural and full of tears . . . After all, to console men there is nothing better than women. I don't know if I am thinking nonsense or writing a sinful phrase, but I do believe that an element of consolation which will always be missing in religious writers, and which exists in the saints I've mentioned, is the voluptuousness of the mystical sentiment.

IV

The works of Sister Emmerich have influenced my soul in a way contrary to what I was hoping. Instead of calming my sorrows of passion they have rekindled them, to the point that my sufferings are now as intense as on the eve of my entrance to the monastery.

So much have I suffered and so much have I cried during these last three days, in fact, that more than once I have been on the point of leaving, returning to Paris and renouncing my ideas of retreat and oblivion, to fly to where Luisa is and forgive her, forgive her sincerely, offering her my whole life for a new kiss, a caress like the caresses of before, letting her dishonor me and convert me into an instrument of laughter and shame, with the condition that she let herself be embraced, let herself be worshipped . . .

And the most curious thing, what most demonstrates that human beings only listen to the advice that fits with their own desires, is that my pride has disappeared almost completely thanks to the advice of the sacred writer . . . Men will mock me? What of it! I mock men even more. The world is despicable and human opinion is worth less than nothing. The love of oneself is hateful and vain. The only thing that must occupy our heart is the love of others, the love of God, the love of those who suffer, the love of a woman . . . oh, Luisa, Luisa, I still adore you!

V

Today I have spoken frankly with my good chaplain: I have explained to him the impression that the works of Sister Emmerich have produced on my soul and told him that at certain moments of solitude, I am afraid of myself.

Despite his apparent simplicity, the good priest had anticipated me.

"All this," he said, "has no importance whatsoever. The saints themselves have passed through crises of sin and cowardice much greater and much more dangerous than your current crisis. The essential thing is not to let oneself become frightened. Lay aside your reading, flee from solitude and pray. If within nine days, upon ending the novena that you must offer to Our Lady of the Victories, your temptations persist, you may return to Paris. For the time being, have a little courage and onward."

I don't know if it's because at the present moment any firm word seems admirable, or because my spiritual director has a great talent as a leader of men, but the fact is that his advice has changed my feelings completely.

Only twenty-four hours after having desired, with all the ardor that I am capable, a criminal kiss, again I feel calm and prepared to fully renounce everything related to my past.

Tomorrow I will begin the novena, and before eight days have passed I will be totally cured. Courage before all!

VI

Tranquility . . . a relative and melancholy tranquility . . . reigns once more in my soul.

I have begun the novena, and without being profoundly religious in the fetishistic sense that my confessor gives to this word, every day when I pass through the beads of my rosary almost mechanically and repeat my too brief prayers, I find an almost simple, even almost monotonous pleasure in humility and obedience that consoles me. In addition, the hours I pass on bended knees in the chapel tire me materially, and material fatigue always helps to calm my nerves.

My confessor comes to see me every morning, but never speaks to me of my sorrows. Today, when I wanted to give to him some details on the current state of my spirits, he begged me to leave the subject for later.

"I am sure," he said to me, "that when Our Lady of the Victories has heard you pray for nine days, the recovery will be complete. Our Lady of the Victories grants all the miracles asked of her."

The unbreakable faith of this priest exerts a true domination over my mood. He seems to me so morally strong, so frank, so simple and good, that when he is by my side I do not even have the courage to suffer, for fear of displeasing him.

The bad thing is that he only comes to see me in the mornings . . . And my fatal hours are those at night . . .

VII

How long the nights are, far away from Paris! I remember that there, near the boulevard, in my little warm and perfumed house, when I couldn't sleep, I would begin to read or meditate. And the hours passed rapidly; and sometimes dawn surprised me with a cigarette between my lips and an image in my mind. Here every night of insomnia lasts an eternity. When I spend four or five hours without sleeping, I feel myself getting older. The only thing that occupies me is prayer, and prayer itself at times only occupies my lips. More than once I have surprised myself thinking of her, Luisa, with affection, almost with desire, and at the same time offering to the Virgin all my soul, the sacrifice of all my freedom and all the tears in my eyes. On other occasions I begin to recite a "salve" and at the end of thirty or forty words I pass, without noticing, to an "Ave Maria."

The truth is that my recovery is not going as quickly as my confessor imagines.

VIII

Tomorrow is the last day of my novena. The Virgin protects me. Today I have been almost happy, and at two or three different moments, I have laughed with enthusiasm thinking of the ridiculous innocence of my fixed ideas. It is six in the afternoon and still I have not thought for a single moment of Luisa.

Poor little one! So that Our Lady is good to me, last night I swore to pardon, from the bottom of my heart, she who has made me suffer so much. After all, she has also suffered, a lot, perhaps as much as me. Why hold onto rancor? No; now I do not retain any bitterness, and even love her more than ever, like a sister of the soul. The Virgin will approve of me.

I think my life in this monastery is going to be very sweet, very tranquil, very joyful.—Later on I will work calmly; I will write something serious, a history of mystical literature, something that is useful to the glory of God and the enlightenment of men.—Who are the religious writers that I can talk about with true enthusiasm? Saint

Teresa is the first, naturally . . . then Sister Emmerich . . . and Saint John of the Cross . . . also Kempis; yes, Kempis is a great counselor despite the fact that, at certain moments of nervous crisis, his phrases do harm; but I will read him again, now that I am cured . . .

The truth is that today I'm not tired. I am happy. There's something in the depths of my heart that seems to move rhythmically, that enlivens me, that encourages me and that gives me life and warmth. What a pleasure it would be to go for a walk in the garden!

IX

Today I finished my novena. Today I've been happy, completely happy.

My confessor spent several hours by my side, he asked me a thousand questions, and upon leaving he said to me:

"We will keep talking; we have a lot of time; I am sure that within ten years, if God does not call us to a better life, we will still see each other here every day."

He is an excellent man, my confessor.

X

I am cured, entirely cured. During the eight days that have passed since I finished my novena until today, no violent image, no strong temptation has disturbed the peace of my soul.

My past appears before my memory like a very old story, almost like an impersonal adventure. Was I truly the lover of Luisa, or was it another . . . one of my friends . . . with me serving her only as confidant?

I sleep well; I have a good appetite; my confessor says I have gained weight; my ideas are balanced.

Once again I have read the *Imitation* and read it with pleasure. Kempis was a sad monk disenchanted with life, who knew how to summarize in a very brief space the essence of all good and divine advice. It seems like a lie that this same book, which is so admirable to me today, was unpleasant to me at another time.

Already I have begun to work. The Superior has allowed me to have sent from Paris some of my favorite books: books of verse in general. So as not to scandalize my good confessor, I have not wished to bring anything but mystic books, the poetries of Fray Luis de León and of Saint John of the Cross, the *Cristiada*, the *Sagesse* by Verlaine, two or three more books of literature and a Littré Dictionary. The name of Littré does not sound agreeably in the monastery, but no one has dared say a word to me. At heart, monks are not as uncompromising as the clergy.

I am satisfied with the first pages that I have written as an introduction to my history of sacred letters. My confessor has read them and told me that they are admirable. The poor saint loves me so tenderly that everything of mine appears to him excellent.

Yesterday he made a very curious observation. When, at a moment of abandon, I thanked him for his great acts of kindness, he became sad and said to me:

"The friendship I have for you, son of mine, is one of my sins, because it contains some pride. I believe (and repent humbly) that within my devotedness for you, there is a great deal of vain sentiment, for having contributed to your salvation."

XI

A very insignificant circumstance has come to destroy many of my illusions about my recovery. No; I am still not cured; the world still exists for me; I still know how to lie, desire and suffer.

Between the pages of one of the books that came from Paris, I found, the day before yesterday, a blonde curl, one of Luisa's curls. At first I thought of giving it to my good adviser; but the truth is I could not. That curl drives me mad with its color of ancient gold, its sad and delicate color of a princess's hair, its perfume, its softness. And, without knowing what I was doing, I kissed it and burned my lips on its strands. Now, after having promised the Virgin that I wouldn't look at it again, that I would give it to the chaplain, I have just covered it with passionate kisses and tears of desire.

My soul, incoherent and weak, finds itself more tormented than ever, without knowing exactly what it desires and what it needs.

. . . Pray a second novena? No, I cannot; I feel without strength. The best is to confess it all to the confes-

sor . . . tomorrow . . . yes, tomorrow . . . after having
breathed the perfume of her hair, all night long . . . the
last time . . . I swear!

XII

I still have not said anything to anyone. But I've been
strong: for two days I have not opened the book in which
that curl is enclosed . . . If my cell were to catch fire all of
a sudden . . . God knows! . . . perhaps then Temptation
would disappear . . . or perhaps I would throw myself
into the flames to save it, or die with it.

The idea of Death presents itself at every moment
before my imagination. My weak soul sees no definitive
refuge but in suicide.

. . . Why do I not kill myself? . . . Out of fear of God?
. . . No; if I do not kill myself it is because I do not want
to leave her alone in the world; out of jealousy, jealousy;
because the possibility that another, after my eternal
journey, could possess her completely, would make me
suffer horribly even after death.

Luisa, Luisa, my poor, my beloved, my adored Luisa,
what should I do at this moment? Why don't you call to
me? . . . If you made me a sign, I would pass over Honor,
despite myself, and go to kiss your lips, kiss your eyes,
kiss your feet, kneel before you . . . cry again after having
cried so much . . . be your slave again . . . Luisa . . . cursed
are you, for I adore you . . .

XIII

I have continued to struggle; I have tried to resist three more days; I cannot. My acts of courage are pure hypocrisies. I cannot . . . and to think that, blinded by vanity, I came to imagine that I only loved her as a sister! . . . and pleaded to the Virgin for my soul! Madness! . . . What attracts me, what makes me forget everything, forgive everything, run to kneel before her, is she herself, the whiteness of her flesh, her perfume, her caresses, her beauty; she, in brief, and my Passion . . . Blessed are you, Luisa!

FREDERICK ROLFE (Baron Corvo) *Amico di Sandro*

FREDERICK ROLFE (Baron Corvo)
An Ossuary of the North Lagoon and Other Stories

JASON ROLFE *An Archive of Human Nonsense*

ROBERT SCHEFFER *Prince Narcissus and Other Stories*

BRIAN STABLEFORD (editor)
Decadence and Symbolism: A Showcase Anthology

BRIAN STABLEFORD (editor) *The Snuggly Satyricon*

BRIAN STABLEFORD *The Insubstantial Pageant*

BRIAN STABLEFORD *Spirits of the Vasty Deep*

BRIAN STABLEFORD *The Truths of Darkness*

COUNT ERIC STENBOCK *Love, Sleep & Dreams*

COUNT ERIC STENBOCK *Myrtle, Rue & Cypress*

COUNT ERIC STENBOCK *The Shadow of Death*

COUNT ERIC STENBOCK *Studies of Death*

MONTAGUE SUMMERS *The Bride of Christ and Other Fictions*

GILBERT-AUGUSTIN THIERRY *Reincarnation and Redemption*

DOUGLAS THOMPSON *The Fallen West*

TOADHOUSE *Gone Fishing with Samy Rosenstock*

TOADHOUSE *Living and Dying in a Mind Field*

RUGGERO VASARI *Raun*

JANE DE LA VAUDÈRE *The Demi-Sexes and The Androgynes*

JANE DE LA VAUDÈRE *The Double Star and Other Occult Fantasies*

JANE DE LA VAUDÈRE *The Mystery of Kama and Brahma's Courtesans*

JANE DE LA VAUDÈRE *The Priestesses of Mylitta*

JANE DE LA VAUDÈRE *Syta's Harem and Pharaoh's Lover*

JANE DE LA VAUDÈRE *Three Flowers and The King of Siam's Amazon*

JANE DE LA VAUDÈRE *The Witch of Ecbatana and The Virgin of Israel*

AUGUSTE VILLIERS DE L'ISLE-ADAM *Isis*

RENÉE VIVIEN AND HÉLÈNE DE ZUYLEN DE NYEVELT
Faustina and Other Stories

RENÉE VIVIEN *Lilith's Legacy*

RENÉE VIVIEN *A Woman Appeared to Me*

KAREL VAN DE WOESTIJNE *The Dying Peasant*